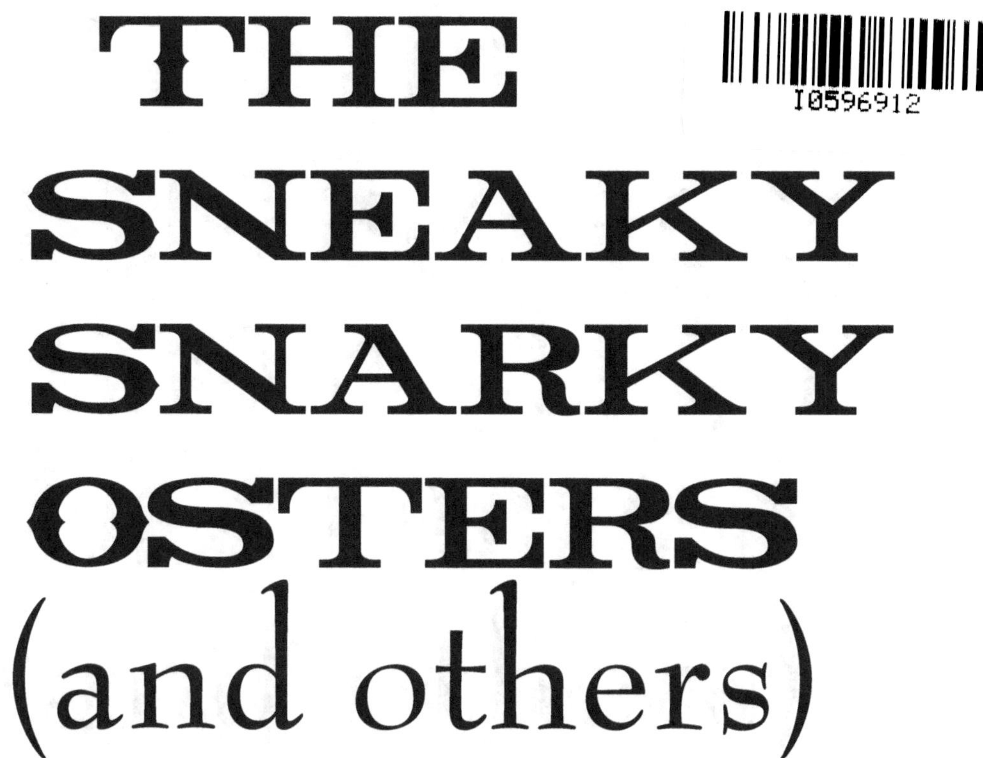

THE SNEAKY SNARKY OSTERS (and others)

A book of 26 poems

by P. Calavara

THE SNEAKY SNARKY OSTERS
(and others)

A book of 26 poems

by P. Calavara

The Sneaky Snarky Osters (and others): A book of 26 poems.

A delicious treatise on rare and unusual creatures by P. Calavara

2016 © P. Calavara & Never Knows Books

This book was written and drawn by P. Calavara, though a couple of the works were created in accordance with the wishes of Thurston Perry, who served as a technical advisor for a couple of the creatures. "You should write a poem about a thing called The Hamster Eater." "Monster Mice make their babies carry stones. Put that in." I think also he named the Osters. Whatever.

The poems were all originally jotted down into a little notebook, and the drawings all exist as ink on bits of paper, all piled up in a corner of my office near the scanner.

ISBN: 978-0-9964120-8-7

P. Calavara is the name of a symbiotic set of twins who endlessly bicker about which one of them is the parasite. They live in Olympia, WA, and take it in turns to misspell words that I swear to God I used to know how to spell just last week.

Never Knows Books is a wholly owned subsidiary of the
Never Knows Heavy Manufacturing Concern.

If you'd like to follow along at home, you may use these links:

Calavara.com § NeverKnows.com

Alister the Alistair

Alister the Alistair
Has spiky teeth and spiky hair
Spiky claws and spiky toes
Spiky eyes and button nose

Alister looks fierce, it's true
And oh the things that she can do
Crushing mountains when she runs
Eating cities just for fun

Alister the Alistair
Would jump when there was nothing there
She'll smash your car just for a lark
She does her best work after dark

Alistairs are prone to drool
They're very, very fond of rules
They never ever make a fuss
Unless, of course, they feel they must

Alister cannot be stayed
But there's no need to be afraid
She's off napping in some daisies
Because Alistairs are very lazy

The Beebebebee

The Beebebebee
Is a behemoth being
Bespectacled, beefy
And besot with bee-stings
Besmirched, bereft
Bejeweled and becoming
It bee-keeps and bemoans
Before all the bee-humming
Its beholden and beaten
Behind and belittled
Benighted, beheld
Bespoke, and bespittled
It's bedazzled beliefs
Bely a beseech
That the Beebebebee
Would rather be at the beach

The Cordial Coggles

The Cordial Coggles
Have wonderful goggles
And love to live under
The bed, the bed, the bed

They're very polite
As they bid you, "goodnight,"
And are incredibly smart and
Well-read, well-read, well-read

They make beautiful hats
For the neighborhood rats
But give them to the mice
Instead, instead, instead

And if you're ever scared
They will brush out your hair
And tell you it's all in
Your head, your head, your head
They'll tell you it's all in your head.

Dave

Dave has fur
And horns and claws
And teeth fill up
His mighty maw

His prey all quiver
At his call
But he only eats bugs
For he's very
    Very
      Very
        Very
          Very
          Small

Edwin

Edwin is mighty
And noble and strong
Incredibly handsome
And never been wrong

He's tall and has muscles
And is nothing but brave
And he is also very
    Very

        Very

            Very

                Very

                    Very

                        Scared of Dave

The Fecks

The Fecks are all fooble
When fiffles are froo
And often with fewtors
As fobby Fecks do

If the flaffy is full
And the fuhfuh is fallow
You can bet that those Fecks
Will flip out in the shallows

They'll fuff up a foody
And feefoil a faboodle
While foomering fannows
Fillyfongfif-a-foodle

Fecks are well-folted
For flippity flouse
Unless you ferfuggle
Your whole foopy house!

Gus

Gus is defiantly diffident and purposefully proud
Catastrophically chatty and languidly loud
Gus is horribly haughty and will defend with his fists
The silliest notions once he's given the gist
Gus snickers and heckles, is remarkably rude
He's bellicose and he bellows, but he's also a prude
Too authoritative by half and the grandest of gits
If you dare ask a question he'll respond with a fit
Gus is the truest of terrors who makes all the kids cry
A vulgarian who fills his mother with pride

The Hamster-Eater

The Hamster-Eater is slimy and scaled
With a fistful of spikes at the end of his tail
His claws are so sharp, his teeth are so red
And he's got four horns growing out of his head

The Hamster-Eater is silent and cunning
Whenever he's seen, most people start running
He sleeps through the day, hunts through the night
And I must say, he looks quite a fright!

But when the Hamster-Eater is getting too near
Fret ye not, for there's nothing to fear
you see he only eats carrots until he gets fat
... I wonder why they call him that?

I, Just The I

I am I, just the I
A fantastical creature
A fifty foot woman
A boy, and a teacher
I'm cowboys, a viking
Artists and the sky
I was once an iguana
But don't ask me why

I am I, just the I
Though I could also be you
And then I could be a beast
Who tells you what to do!
I was a gnome and a king
And I once was a cat
Though that was a bore
Since all I did was nap

I am I, just the I
And I rage when I'm mad
And whenever that's through
Worlds end when I'm sad
Whenever I'm happy
I put stars in the sky
My laughter is magic
Because I am the I

I am I, just the I
I'm a doctor, a mouse
I once kissed a llama
And jumped over a house
I'm the greatest guitarist
And I've been to the moon
I once fought a lion
And I'm quite the raccoon

I am I, just the I
I fight monsters for fun
Until I switch roles
And the heroes all run
I'm the wind and the rain
I'm the happy, the pain
I'm the praise and complain
I'm the strength and the wain

I am I, just the I
Just a nebulous thing
All parts and potential
Tied up with a string
I am I, just the I
Just whatever I said
Just a whim and a whimper
And a thought in my head

Joanne and the Jobots

Joanne made some robots
And called them *the Jobots*
Then she taught them to do lots of stuff

She showed them how to walkbot
They learned how to talkbot
And to wear clothes so they weren't in the buff

She taught them how to dancebot
They all loved to prancebot
And they learned to make jokes off the cuff

She had them do all her mathbot
And they took all her bathsbot
For playing cards she showed them how to bluff

She taught them not to be boresbot
And to do all her choresbot
And gave them tattoos to show how they were tough

They were made to say pleasebot
And to eat all her peasbot
And she decided, "Well, that's good enough."

The Kiffers

Everyone says to see a Kiffer
For as you know they have great horns
Horns as tall as trees
And strong as mountains are the norm

Horns that stretch in angles
Horns that curve with simple grace
A Kiffer's horns are so amazing
That they're visible from space

People flock in masses
To get a glimpse at Kiffer horns
And there's quite a celebration
When a new Kiffer is born

Be sure you've got a camera
With a big wide-angle lens
And stand back a thousand feet
And then a thousand more again

In fact, step back another thousand
The Kiffers sure won't mind
For they'd like a little privacy
If you would just be so kind

The Lump

The Lump is my town's superhero
We all think that he's just the best
And he'd be out stopping villains right now
If he wasn't at home for a rest

The Lump is a master detective
He'll gather up all of the clues
And then sort them all out like a puzzle
As soon as he's finished his snooze

If some dastardly fiend robs a bank
You can bet that the Lump will be there
And that he'll stay at the bank for the day
For the bank has the comfiest chairs

If some madman has threatened the city
And looks like he's ready to snap
The Lump will be right there to save us
But first he just needs a quick nap

Yes, the Lump is my town's superhero
The greatest hero of our time
The only way that our town could be safer
Is if he turned to a life full of crime

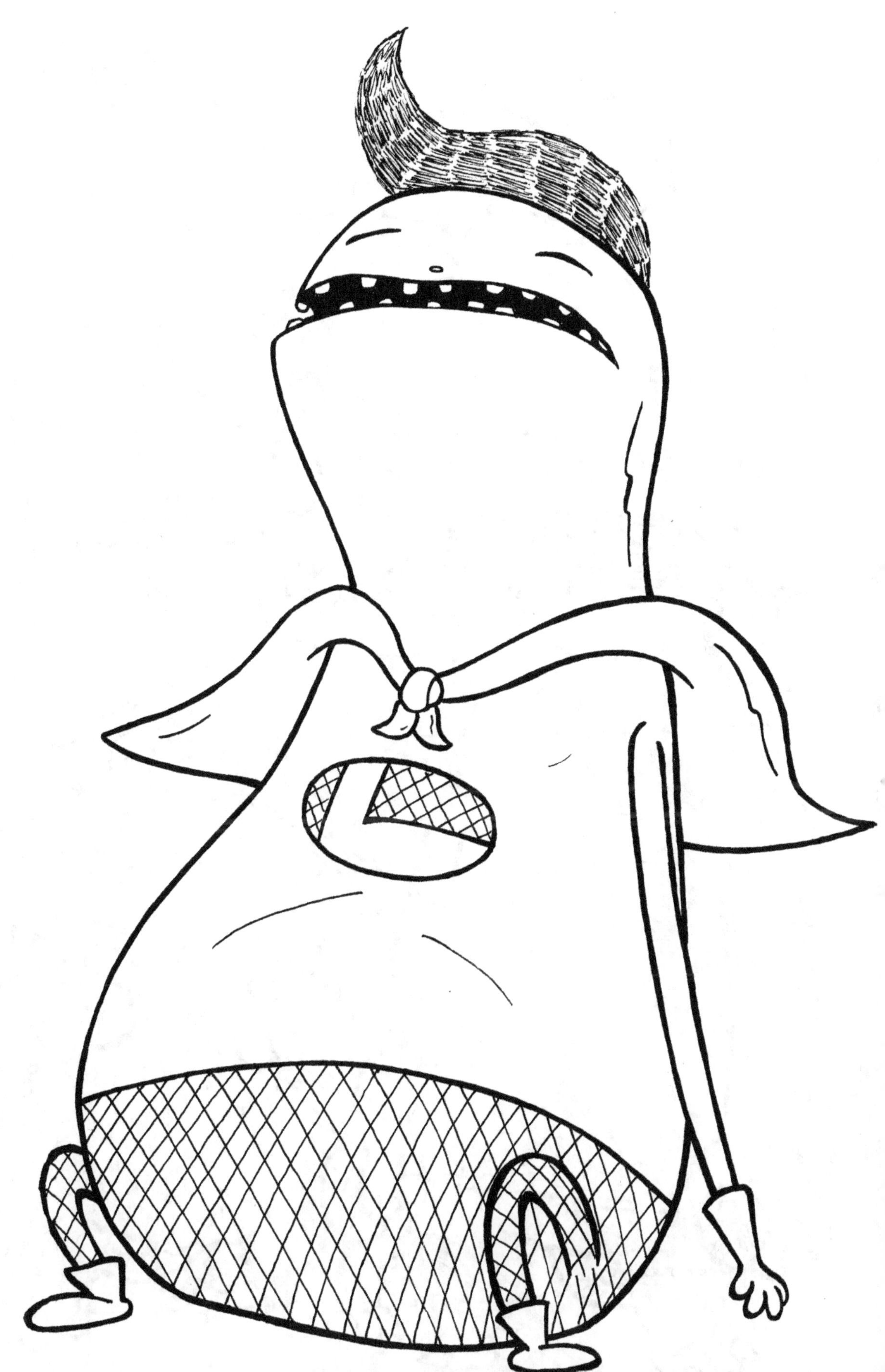

Monster Mice

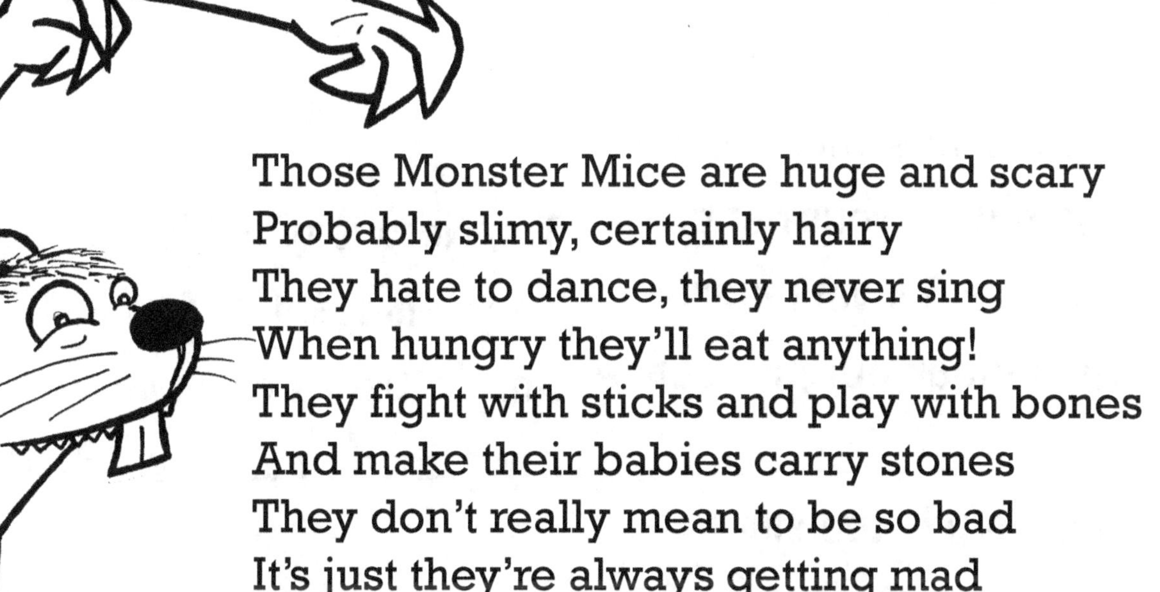

Those Monster Mice are huge and scary
Probably slimy, certainly hairy
They hate to dance, they never sing
When hungry they'll eat anything!
They fight with sticks and play with bones
And make their babies carry stones
They don't really mean to be so bad
It's just they're always getting mad
They chase the kids and dads get spanked
They yell at moms and dogs are ranked
And while it's true they're mean and such
The worst thing is they fart too much

The Nerp

The Nerp is coming!
The Nerp is coming!
All smooth like a frog
And probably humming

She'll burgle your dresser
And put on your pants
She'll eat all your socks
Then break out in a dance

The Nerp is too silly
She never acts normal
She's frequently nude
And always too formal

She'll steal your apples
And teach all your fish
To cuss just like sailors
If that's what you wish

The Nerp is gigantic
She's pleasant and round
And as big as a whale
If weighed pound by pound

She'll throw all your toys
Up onto your roof
And then when you shout
She will get all aloof

The Nerp is coming!
My parents are worried
The Nerp is coming!
And I do wish she'd hurry

The Osters

The sneaky snarky Osters
Plot to perpetrate and foster
The pernicious provocation that they're bad

For the secret that they're hiding
Beneath all their crass conniving
Is that the sneaky snarky Osters are all rad

The Piggles

The Piggles are not pigs who are biggle
Nor are they pigs who are tiggles
They're definitely not pigs with the giggles
And certainly aren't pigs who love figgles
They assure that they're not pigs who wiggle
And I assume they're not pigs who are swiggled
So what do we make of these Piggles?
Well, my friend, they are pigs who love Quiggles

The Quiggles

Quiggles are quaint
And quick to insist
They're quite sure
They don't know
That the Piggles exist

The Ree

Have you ever considered the Ree?
It's like a dinosaur crossed with a tree!
And if you were to ask me,
It's a thing you should certainly see!

Sarah

Sarah the strongest most savage and smartest
Stuck her tongue at whatever mom said

So Sarah the strongest most savage and smartest
Skipped dinner and went straight to bed

The Twurp

The Twurp is a bully
He's orange and he's mean
He likes to kick puppies
He only wants green

The Twurp will laugh cruelly
Whenever you're down
And that thing on his head
Makes him look like a clown

The Twurp cannot read
Except for his name
Which he sprays onto things
That he wishes to claim

The Twurp's a know-nothing
He's never done work
If you ask him a question
His response is a smirk

The Twurp's ego's too big
As his claws are too small
and "Pay attention to me!"
Is the Twurp's mating call

The Twurp is so fatuous
That what else can I say?
Perhaps if we ignore him
He will just go away

Umm

The other kids have fabulous beasts
Like Speckled Grells and Palimokeests
But me, I am stuck with an Umm
Ho hum

There are Flying Hillies with flaming tails
And Rombotromps as big as whales
But me, I am stuck with an Umm
That bum

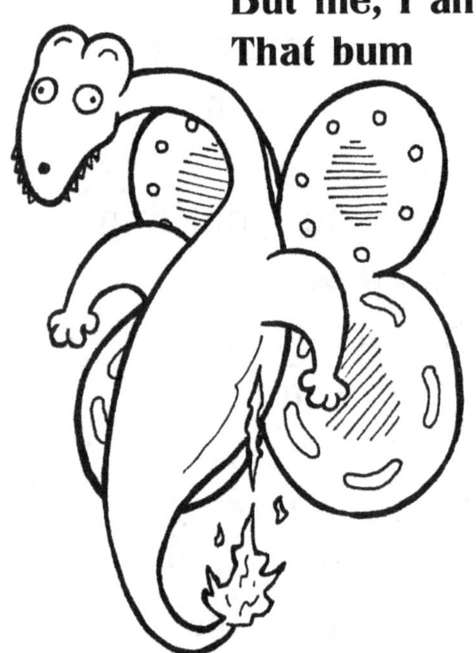

The Lurching Flipples yearn to sing
And everyone knows of the wise Vladderfings
But me, I am stuck with an Umm
How dumb

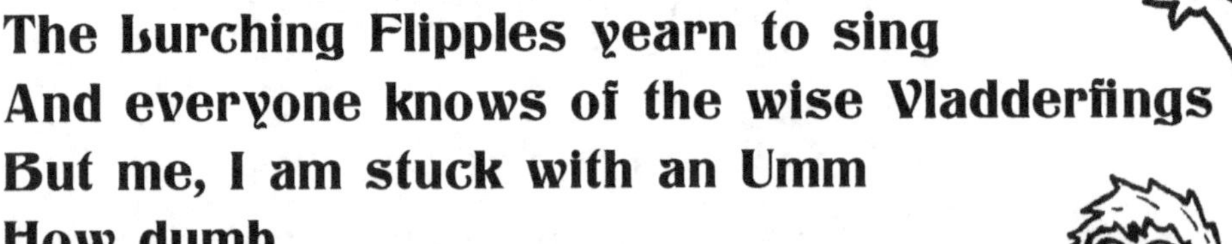

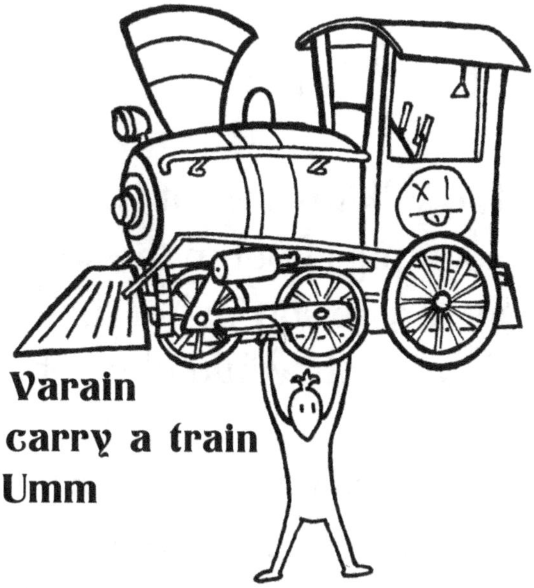

I begged my dad to adopt a Varain
A creature so strong it can carry a train
But me, I am stuck with an Umm
Humdrum

I would even love to have a Kerfilly
A monster so goofy it only acts silly
But me, I am stuck with an Umm
How come?

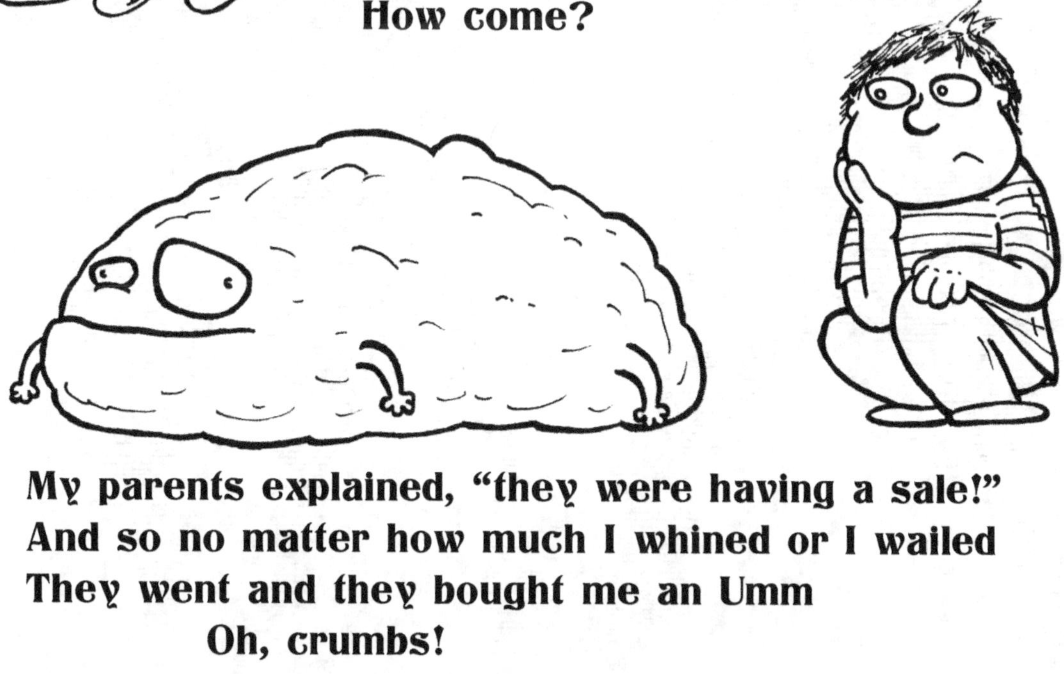

My parents explained, "they were having a sale!"
And so no matter how much I whined or I wailed
They went and they bought me an Umm
Oh, crumbs!

The Villains

The Villains are out there tonight
Roaming about in the street
Be sure to stay out of their sight
Unless you would like to be beat

They travel in groups or alone
They carry sharp knives and their fists
You should run straight off to your home
If you see them step out of the mist

The Villains are out there tonight
The best thing to do is to hide
They'll be out there until the first light
When they'll vanish and go back inside

They're probably coming right now
But you're safe so there's no need to shout
And if you are wondering how
Thank your parents for keeping them out

The Wipple-Bown-Wollies

The Wipple-Bown-Wollies
All call themselves Molly
And are frequently found at the zoo

And whenever they meet
They exclaim, "That's so neat!
I'm Molly, too! How do you do?"

The Xuixookalompatoose

The Xuixookalompatoose
Has such a hard name
That the poem about it
Must be short and inane

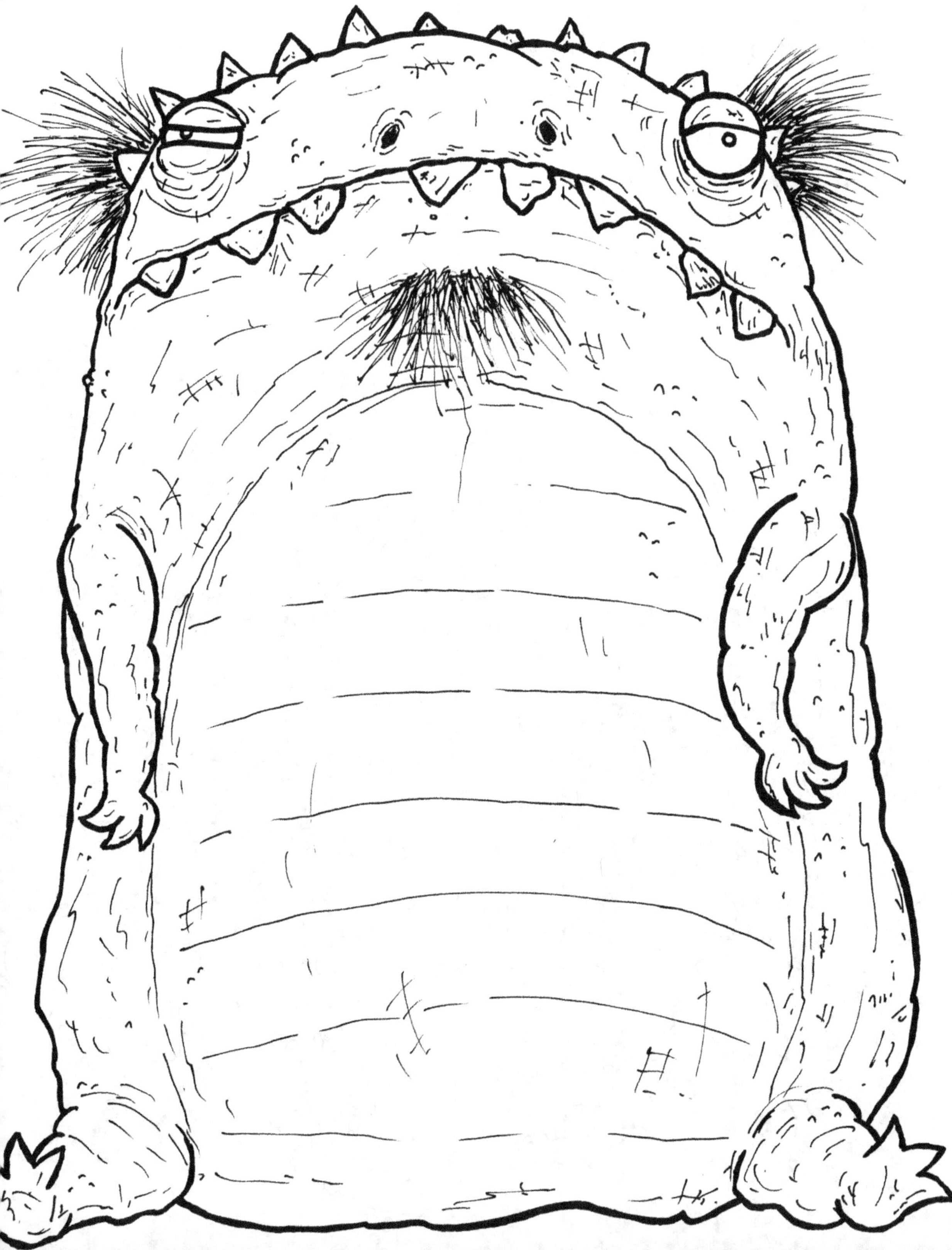

Yuffies

Yuffies are fluffy
Adorably scruffy
With chins never stubbly
And eyes that are bubbly
Cheeks full of dimples
But never with pimples
With cute little noses
They smell just like roses

Their hands are petite
And they're neat when they eat
Always sharply dressed
And they're never a mess
The Yuffies are soft
And are always well-washed
But despite what you thought
Cute? BOY, *THEY ARE NOT!*

The Zapple Crabs

The Zapple Crabs are zapple mad
And zapple bad and zapple sad

They're zapple cruel and zapple sappy
Zapple rude and zapple happy

They're zapple blue, they zapple think
That they would like a zapple drink

They're zapple tired and zapple whine
When things are not all zapple fine

They zapple hope, they zapple eat
And zapple run on zapple feet

They zapple talk and zapple creep
But for some reason they pazzle sleep

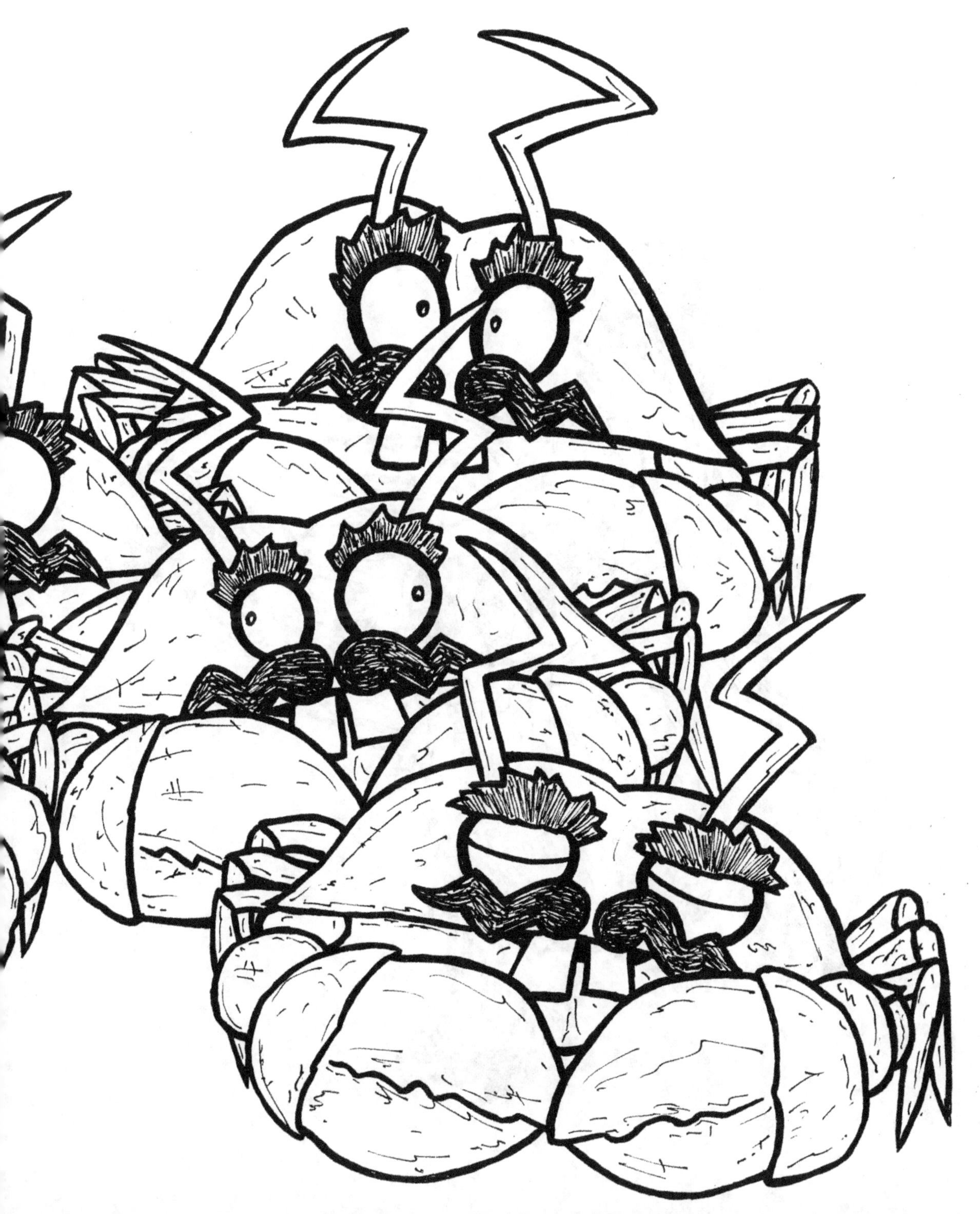